# By Dorie McCullough Lawson

Trafalgar Square
North Pomfret, Vermont

For the Tate Family of Wymont Ranch

**This is Luke.**

He lives in a house near the ocean
with his mother, his father,
his big sister, his big brother,
his little sister and his two dogs.

But Luke imagines he is...

**Tex.**

**Tex loves mountains**

**and wide open spaces.**

Tex works at the Wymont Ranch.

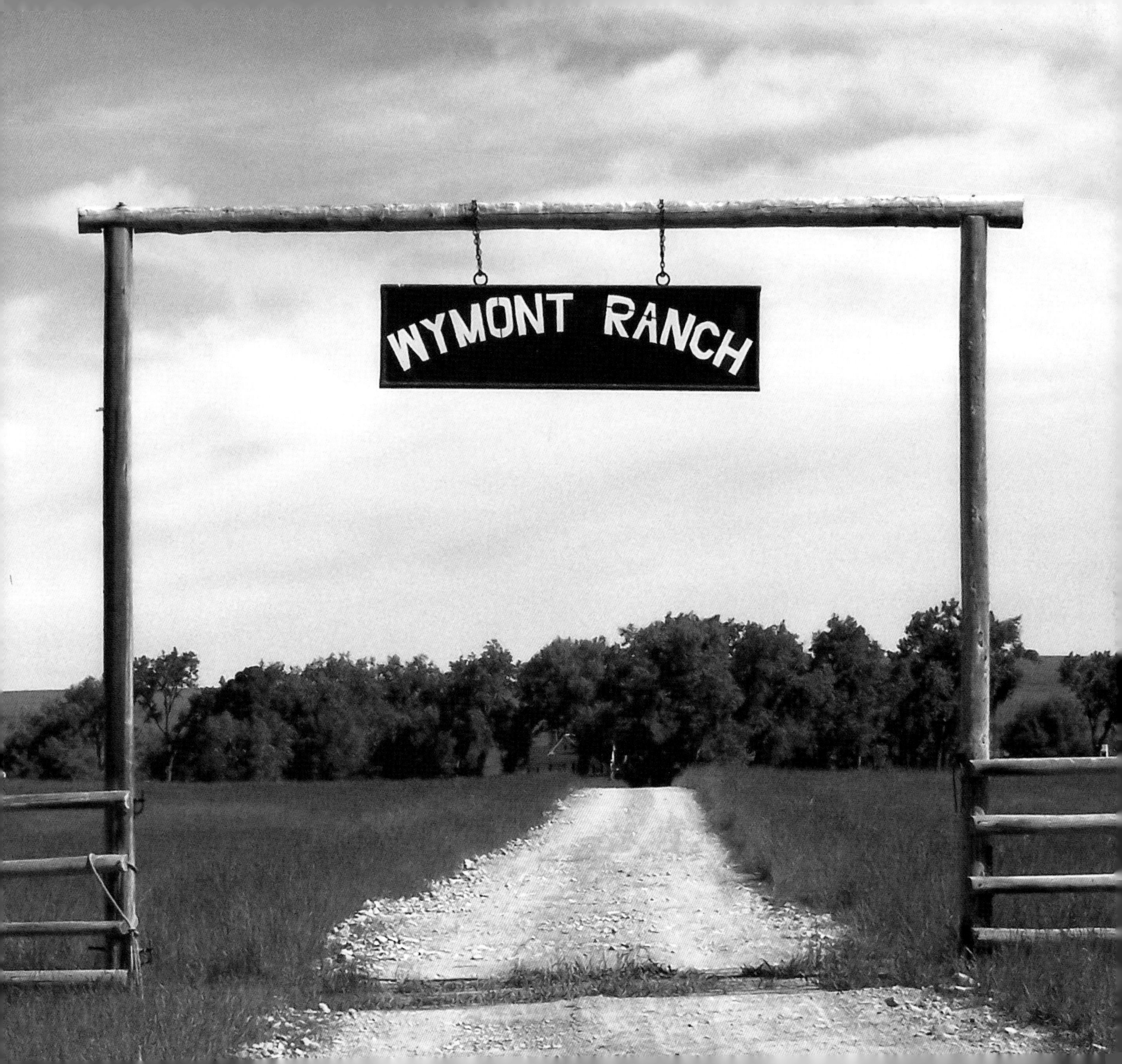
WYMONT RANCH

He sleeps in the bunkhouse.

He has a good old cowdog named Sue.

**All day long Tex works hard.**

**He rides.**

He irrigates.

He checks fence.

He rounds up the herd.

**Sometimes Tex works with Cowboy Jim.**

Tex takes good care of his horse, Thunder.

**Thunder is Tex's best friend.**

Sometimes Tex even brings Thunder
into the ranch house!

**Then it's back outside for more work.**

**And a little rest.**

It's been a long day for a cowboy.

So long, Tex.

Good night, Luke.

*Tex* only came to be because of significant help from the following:
Mimi Tate, Dick Tate, Alex Oakes, Jim Smith, Hardy Tate, Laura MacCarty,
Melissa McDonald, Kathy Wipfler, Rob Beckman, Steve Gage, the late Allen
Anderson, Cindy Lang, Chuck Neustifter, Frank and Rita Hagan, Melissa
Marchetti, Mike Hill, David and Rosalee McCullough, Rebecca Didier,
Martha Cook, Caroline Robbins, Rosie Lawson, Nathaniel Lawson,
Luke Lawson, May Lawson, Honey Pooh, Bumblebee, Duke,
Annie, Sue, Rumple, Sabrina,
and above all, Tim Lawson.

First published in 2011 by
Trafalgar Square Books
North Pomfret, Vermont 05053

Printed in China

Copyright © 2011 Dorie McCullough Lawson

Library of Congress Cataloging-in-Publication Data
Lawson, Dorie McCullough.
Tex / by Dorie McCullough Lawson.
p. cm.
ISBN 978-1-57076-501-8
I. Title.
PZ7.L43824Te 2011
[E]--dc23
2011014775

Book and cover design by RM Didier

Typefaces: Wembley, Gill Sans

10 9 8 7 6 5 4 3 2 1